Rabén & Sjögren Stockholm

Translation copyright © 1995 by Rabén & Sjögren
All rights reserved
Originally published in Sweden by Rabén & Sjögren
under the title *Ellen*,
pictures and text copyright © 1994 by Catarina Kruusval
Library of Congress catalog card number: 95-067922
Printed in Italy
First edition, 1995

ISBN 91 29 63074 6

Catarina Kruusval

NO CLOTHES TODAY!

R&S
BOOKS

Stockholm   New York   London   Adelaide   Toronto

Ellen is in a bad mood.

Ellen doesn't want to wear the green sweater.
But maybe …

Kitty wants to.

Ellen doesn't want to wear the check dress.
But maybe ...

Teddy wants to.

Ellen doesn't want the red ribbon.
But maybe ...

the bunny wants it.

Ellen doesn't want the black shoes.
But maybe …

the elephant wants them.

Ellen doesn't want to wear the
flowered undershirt. But maybe ...

Buster does.

Ellen doesn't want to wear the striped socks.
But maybe …

the doll wants to.

Ellen doesn't want to wear her pants.
But maybe ...

the pig does.

Then Ellen finds Grandpa's
nice big hat ...

That's what Ellen wants to wear!

Ellen gets the pig with her pants ...

and the doll with the striped socks.

She gets Buster and Kitty ...

and the elephant with the black shoes.

Ellen　gets the bunny with the red ribbon ...

and Teddy with the check dress.
Now everyone is here. But where is Ellen?

Here she is!
And now Ellen is happy.